LITTLE TIGER PRESS LTD,
an imprint of the Little Tiger Group
1 Coda Studios, 189 Munster Road, London SW6 6AW
Imported into the EEA by Penguin Random House Ireland,
Morrison Chambers, 32 Nassau Street, Dublin D02 YH68
www.littletiger.co.uk

First published in Great Britain 2020
This edition published 2021

A CIP catalogue record for this book is available from the British Library

Printed in China • LTP/1800/4763/0322

4 6 8 10 9 7 5

For Caoilte and Aoibheanna
~ C G

For Solar x
~ T W

This Little Tiger book belongs to:

_____

_____

_____

A Little Bit Worried

Ciara Gavin

Tim Warnes

LITTLE TIGER

LONDON

Weasel was minding his own business,
out collecting leaves,
when suddenly the weather changed.

Weasel was **soaked** through by a nasty rain.

Then a gust of wind **knocked him**

FLAT on his bottom.

Weasel stood up and puffed out his chest.
"That's *enough* of that messing,"
he told the sky.

But just then the heavens opened up
and he was bumped about by a mighty hail shower.

Weasel was starting to feel very small
and defenceless against this angry storm.

He built a wall to keep him safe.
But the gale blew in and it
whirled around all night.

So, he built the wall **higher**.

But then the rain came back and wouldn't
take no for an answer.

So, Weasel made a roof.
"Keep out,"
he said, satisfied.

Weasel settled down in his new safe place.
He thought of the storm raging outside and
it made him shiver.

Time passed,
and Weasel got used
to being by himself.
But one day, he turned
around . . .

. . . and was alarmed to find Mole
sitting on his couch.

"What is this place?" asked Mole.

"It's a fortress,"
said Weasel nervously.
"Oh, marvellous,"
nodded Mole.
"I love a good fortress.
You guard this side and
I'll guard that one."

"No!" said Weasel.

"It's not for playing in. It's a home."

"Marvellous," yawned Mole, getting comfortable. "Pop the kettle on."

"No!" fretted Weasel.
"It's not a place for visitors!
It's a place to hide."

"Marvellous,"
said Mole.

"You count to
ten and I'll hide,
no peeking!"

"No!" insisted Weasel.

"It's not for **games!**
It's for keeping me safe."

"Who's after you?"
asked Mole. "Is it Fox?
He's a wily one.
I'll help scare him off.
Look at my
scary face."

"No," groaned Weasel. "I'm hiding from the storm
and there isn't room for the both of us."

"Well, where's the fun in that?"
replied Mole.

"It's not meant to
be fun!" said Weasel.
"Just safe."

"Well, what's wrong with a good storm anyway?" added Mole, placing a hand on Weasel's shoulder.

Weasel told Mole about the wind
and the rain, the damp and the chill,
the snow and the ice.
All the things that frightened him most.

"The storm is scary," sighed Weasel.
"And much, much **bigger** than me."

"I see," said Mole gently.
"But storms can be such fun, too!
Whenever it snows, I love to scoop it up
and make a snowman."

"And the **wind**," questioned Weasel, "that **knocks** you off your feet?"

"Oh, I love when that happens!" beamed Mole.

"The wind lifts my fur and it feels all **ticklish**."

With a giggle, he **twirled** and fell over laughing.

"But the cold rain, Mole," continued Weasel,
"what do you do when you get caught in *that?*"

"Why, I splash about in the biggest puddles
I can find!" replied Mole.

"Then, I sit in an armchair by
the fire and dry off with a cup of hot soup.
Soup always tastes *extra* wonderful
when you've been out in the rain."

Mole had such a different
way of seeing things.

"But Mole," said Weasel,
"what do you do when you feel
afraid to face something?"

"I face it with my friend," smiled Mole.
And with that, he held out his hand.

Weasel took Mole's hand,
and together they walked out
into a warm, sunny day.